To read fluently is one of the basic aims of anyone learning English as a foreign language. **And it's never too early to start.** Ladybird Graded Readers are interesting but simple stories designed to encourage children between the ages of 6 and 10 to read with pleasure.

Reading is an excellent way of reinforcing language already acquired, as well as broadening a child's vocabulary. Ladybird Graded Readers use a limited number of grammatical structures and a carefully controlled vocabulary, but where the story demands it, a small number of words outside the basic vocabulary are introduced. In *The Enormous Turnip* the following words are outside the basic vocabulary for this grade:

boots, enormous, mouse, plant, pull up, turnip

Further details of the structures and vocabulary used at each grade can be found in the Ladybird Graded Readers *leaflet.*

A list of books in the series can be found on the back cover.

British Library Cataloguing in Publication Data

Ullstein, Sue
    The enormous turnip. — (English language teaching series).
    1. English language — Text-books for foreign speakers
    2. Readers — 1950-
    I. Title   II. Dyke, John   III. Series
    428.64   PE1128
    ISBN 0-7214-1038-3

First edition

Published by Ladybird Books Ltd Loughborough Leicestershire UK
Ladybird Books Inc Lewiston Maine 04240 USA

© LADYBIRD BOOKS LTD MCMLXXXVII

Printed in England

The Enormous Turnip

written by Sue Ullstein
illustrated by John Dyke

Ladybird Books

This old man has
some seeds. They are
turnip seeds.

The old man plants
the seeds.

He waters the seeds.

The turnip seeds
grow.

One turnip grows
and
grows
and
grows!

It is
enormous!

"I'm hungry,"
the old man says.
"I must pull up
the enormous turnip.
We can have it for
supper."

He puts on his boots.

He pulls the turnip.
He pulls and pulls,
but he cannot pull up
the enormous turnip.

The old man calls to
the old woman.

"Come and help me!"
he says. "I want to
pull up this enormous
turnip."

The old woman pulls the old man, and the old man pulls the turnip. They pull and pull, but they cannot pull up the enormous turnip.

The old woman calls to a boy.

"Come and help us," she says. "We want to pull up this enormous turnip."

The boy pulls the old woman. The old woman pulls the old man, and the old man pulls the turnip. They pull and pull, but they cannot pull up the enormous turnip.

The boy calls to a girl.

"Come and help us!"
he says. "We want
to pull up
this enormous turnip."

The girl pulls the boy.
The boy pulls the old
woman. The old
woman pulls the old
man, and the old man
pulls the turnip.

They pull and pull, but
they cannot pull up
the enormous turnip.

The girl calls to a dog.

"Come and help us!" she says. "We want to pull up this enormous turnip."

The dog pulls the girl.
The girl pulls the boy.
The boy pulls the old
woman. The old
woman pulls the old
man, and the old man
pulls the turnip.

They pull and pull, but they cannot pull up the enormous turnip.

The dog calls to a cat.

"Come and help us!" he says. "We want to pull up this enormous turnip."

The cat pulls the dog.
The dog pulls the girl.
The girl pulls the boy.
The boy pulls the old
woman. The old
woman pulls the old
man, and the old man
pulls the turnip.

They pull and pull, but
they cannot pull up
the enormous turnip.

The cat calls to a
mouse.

"Come and help us!"
she says. "We want to
pull up this enormous
turnip."

The mouse pulls the cat. The cat pulls the dog. The dog pulls the girl. The girl pulls the boy. The boy pulls the old woman.

The old woman pulls
the old man, and the
old man pulls the
turnip. They pull and
pull and…

the enormous turnip
comes **up**!

They carry the turnip
home.

And they have turnip for supper.